WELCOME TO Pump Street Primary

Meet some of the children ...

Barry Barsby

Daisy Poborski

Rashid Ali

Floella Potts

Danny Bloor

Monica Bellis

... in Miss Twigg's class

Craig Soapy

Karen Smart

Terry Flynn

Fatima Patel

Lily Wongsam

Paul Dimbley

Titles in the Pump Street Primary series

THIS IS BOB WILSON

He wrote this story
and drew the pictures.

He lives in the Derbyshire countryside in a house which he designed and built himself from an old cowshed. He has three grown-up children and nine grandchildren. When he was young he wanted to be a pop star, and he started to write songs. He became an art teacher and wrote plays and musicals, and shows for television and radio. Then he began to write and illustrate stories for children. He is the author of the *Stanley Bagshaw* picture books and the best-selling *Ging Gang Goolie, It's an Alien!*

For Mark
Have fun!
Bob Wilson

First published 2001 by Macmillan Children's Books
a division of Pan Macmillan Limited
20 New Wharf Road, London N1 9RR
Basingstoke and Oxford
www.panmacmillan.com

Associated companies throughout the world

ISBN 0 330 39819 9

1 3 5 7 9 8 6 4 2

A CIP catalogue record for this book is available from
the British Library.

Printed and bound in Great Britain by Mackays of Chatham plc, Kent

Visit Bob Wilson's website at www.planetbob.co.uk

Daring Dan

written and illustrated by
Bob Wilson

MACMILLAN CHILDREN'S BOOKS

Here are some of the school staff ...

Mr C Warrilow BSc MEd

Miss Twigg

Mr Manley

Mr Boggis

Mrs York

Mr Lamp-Williams

Miss Gaters

Mrs Jellie

Norman Loops

Janice

Mrs Brazil

For Ami, Thomas, Elias,
Matilda, Reuben, Alexander,
Marius, Lucien and Babik

THIS IS DANNY BLOOR

(and a bunch of flowers).
Dan isn't like the other boys in our class.
He's different.

Miss Twigg, our class teacher, calls him
her little treasure.

Craig, Terry, Barry and Mark call him
something else.
(At least they used to.)

Most boys in our class have interesting and exciting hobbies.
For example, Barry and Mark collect picture cards of rare Japanese monsters.

And Craig and Terry spend their spare time dodging dragons in dark dangerous dungeons.

But Dan Bloor likes to play on his own.
And *his* hobbies are *really boring*.
For example, he collects things for
Mr Warrilow's
nature table.

This is a barn owl's feather.
Where did you find it?

On the roof of
an old barn.

And he does embroidery!

A few weeks ago Dan brought some of his embroidery into school. Miss Twigg asked him to stand on a chair and hold it up for us all to see.

Julie thought it was lovely.
Lily said she thought Dan was very clever.
Barry, Terry, Craig and Mark didn't say anything at all. They just smirked.
But we all knew what they were thinking.

But they don't think that now.
Not after what happened at the Black
Pig Mine. If you were to ask them
now what they thought of Danny Bloor
they'd say,
"*He's a star!*"
"*He's a mate.*"
"*He's got what it takes!*"
Because when Mrs Batty lost her dog,
when we nearly got struck by lightning,
and might have been attacked by an
enraged rabbit, when everybody else
was *really really scared*,
Danny Bloor did something

Really
Really
DARING!

(EVEN MORE DARING THAN WHEN BARRY BARSBY
PUT A WHOOPEE CUSHION ON THE HEADMASTER'S CHAIR.)

IT STARTED LIKE THIS

Miss Twigg was telling us about the olden days.

She said that in the olden days ordinary people didn't have the things we have today like videos and televisions and computer games.

> **What did they *do* all day?**

said Craig.

"They worked," said Miss Twigg.
"They worked long hours in the mines and the mills and the factories.
It was a hard life.
But the men who owned the mines and the mills and the factories had a problem too.
Their problem was they didn't have . . ."

A PROPERLY DEVELOPED COMMUNICATION NETWORK

Nobody had any idea what this meant
(except for Karen Smart).
Karen said,

It means they didn't have mobile phones.

"Crikey!" said Terry. "That must have
been terrible."

Supposing your dad was a mine owner
and he was stuck in a traffic jam the other
side of Luton airport because a lorry had
spilled its load on the motorway.
How could he let your mum know that
he'd be late home for tea?
What would he do, Karen?

Shout.

Miss Twigg said it was true. They *didn't*
have mobile phones in the olden days.
But that wasn't the problem.
Miss Twigg said what she should have
written on the flip chart was

THE ROADS WERE NOT VERY GOOD

And that was why the canals were built.
The canals were used to carry raw
materials from the mines and quarries
and farms in the country to the factories
in the towns and cities. Once upon a
time the canals were like motorways are
today.
The canals are a living relic of our
industrial past. And that was why, as
part of our history project, we were
going on a trip along

THE BURSTON
AND
CLEAM CANAL

Miss Twigg had a leaflet.
She read it out to us. She said,
"Listen to this. I think it sounds really interesting."

It was built to serve the copper mines at Cleam ...
It has been painstakingly restored ...
It gives a unique insight into the life and work of the miners and canal folk.

We thought it sounded really boring.

But Miss Twigg insisted that we should be prepared for an 'educational adventure along one of Britain's most historic waterways'.
Then she drew a big map on the board to show us where we were going and what we were going to see.

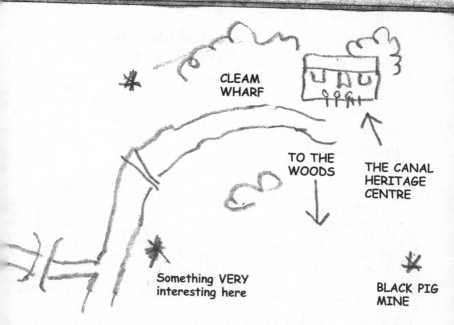

CLEAM
WHARF

TO THE
WOODS

THE CANAL
HERITAGE
CENTRE

Something VERY
interesting here

BLACK PIG
MINE

Karen thought it was very interesting.
Paul thought Miss Twigg was very
clever.
Barry, Terry, Craig and Mark didn't say
anything.
They were thinking.

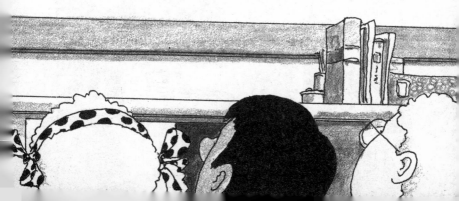

IT WAS THE DAY OF THE TRIP

We were all very excited.
Miss Twigg had said we should be
prepared for an educational adventure
along one of Britain's most historic
waterways. *And we were.* Some were
more prepared than others.
For example,

Barry was wearing swimming goggles
and had brought his pump-action
mega-blaster water pistol.

In case we need to fight
off an enemy submarine.

Craig had come in his camouflaged flak jacket and had brought his brother's mobile phone.

In case we sink and need to be rescued by an army helicopter.

And Danny Bloor was wearing . . .

. . . his duffle coat.

And had brought his mum's umbrella.

Miss Twigg thought that Dan was very
wise to come in his duffle coat and
bring his mum's umbrella.
(*You can probably imagine what Craig
and Terry thought.*)

Our boat was called

THE BURSTON
BLUEBELL

When we were all aboard and in our
seats Miss Twigg gave us each a sheet of
paper.

You are to look out for interesting
things in, on, or near the canal.
If you see something unusual you
must write down what you think it
is – *or might have been.*

We were to be 'historical detectives',
looking for clues to our industrial past.

Miss Twigg said we were going on a canal trip that we would remember for years to come.
She said if we kept our eyes peeled we would see something very interesting and unusual.
And she was right.

Lily Wongsam still talks about it.

We arrived at Cleam Wharf.

As we got off the boat we handed our papers to Karen Smart.

Karen had been chosen to make a list of all the things we'd seen, and to read it out to Miss Twigg.

Miss Twigg said she was looking forward to hearing what Karen had to say.

> The things we observed on our voyage along the Burston and Cleam canal were ...

A cow, some bullrushes, a set of pram wheels, a broken milk crate, a bicycle inner-tube, 58 soft drink cans, an old mattress, a dead cat, three supermarket trolleys, a burst football, what looked like a pair of pink underpants hanging on a barbed wire fence and a duck.

Oh ... and Barry Barsby says he observed a dead werewolf wearing a Rolling Stones T-shirt but to be honest I think it was actually a fisherman with a beard who'd been drinking a beer and fallen asleep.

Miss Twigg seemed a bit disappointed. She said, "Did you not notice anything of *historical* interest?"

"You mean *old*, Miss?" said Rashid Ali.

"Yes," said Miss Twigg.

"I noticed an old wooden building," said Daisy Poborski.

"Good," said Miss Twigg. "What did you think it was, Daisy?"

"An old wooden building," said Daisy.

"Yes. I know that's what it is *now*," said Miss Twigg. "But try to imagine what it must have been like hundreds of years ago when this canal was a busy industrial highway serving mines, factories and farms.

What d'you think that old wooden building was when it was first built?"

"Please, Miss. I know!" said Nicola.

It was a *new* wooden building!

Apparently we had failed to notice

Tranter's Mill

A building of Great
Historical Importance

"Oh, well. Never mind," said Miss Twigg.

Next we were going to have a guided
tour of the Canal Heritage Museum
where we would discover

... a treasure trove of canal
and mining memorabilia,
historical documents, and
exciting educational exhibits.

Miss Twigg was sure that we'd find *at
least something* we could get interested,
excited and enthusiastic about in the
Canal Heritage Museum.

And we did.

Terry and Mark were particularly interested in

A fibre-glass fishing rod with a breaking strain of over 100 kilograms.

Barry and Craig were particularly
enthusiastic about

A walkie-talkie radio
with a range of over
2,000 metres.

And Danny Bloor got really excited by . . .

The assistant said,

She thought it was very good value.
Dan thought it was wonderful.
(*You can imagine what Terry and Mark and Barry and Craig thought.*)

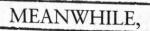

MEANWHILE,

the museum guide was giving Miss Twigg a guided tour.

She wore the same headscarf for over 60 years.

That's interesting. Isn't it, children?

Oi! *You lot*! Over here. *This* is what you're supposed to be looking at.

What we were supposed to be looking at was . . .
a tin water jug, a decorated teapot, and some old photographs of old women wearing old headscarves standing on old canal boats looking miserable.

But Barry Barsby had wandered off.
And he found something to look at that
was *really* interesting.

Now, what's
this about?

It was an old book.
It was called

Myths and Legends
of the Burston and
Cleam Canal

And it was all about

GHOSTS!

We were all interested in the book that Barry had found.
Except for Miss Twigg. She might have told him to stop messing about but the museum guide said, "That's a very interesting book indeed."

The lady who wrote it lives not far from here.

If you want to hear some really strange tales you need to talk to Mrs Batty in person.

Old Mrs Batty lived up in the woods
near the Black Pig Mine.
Her family had been there for hundreds
of years.
"You should go and see Mrs Batty,"
said the museum guide.
"She can tell you tales that will make
your skin crawl."
"Now, listen here," said Miss Twigg.
"We came here to learn about history,
not to—"
Then she suddenly stopped.
She stopped because she'd just thought
of something.

When Miss Twigg had been training to
be a teacher she'd been given a very
useful book. It was called

A GUIDE FOR TRAINEE TEACHERS

Miss Twigg had just remembered what
it had said in chapter 7.

CHAPTER 7

CHILD INTEREST-LED LEARNING

Tests have shown that the concentration span of the average seven-year-old is akin to that of an absent-minded fruit fly. A teacher should therefore not be at all surprised if her class becomes distracted by something which has nothing to do with the lesson in hand. A good teacher will respond to any distraction positively, by turning it into a CHILD-CENTRED, PUPIL-DRIVEN, ON-TASK-INITIATED, INTERACTIVE EDUCATION, LEARNING OPPORTUNITY.

Any Questions?

Q Yes. I took my class on a canal trip so they could learn about history but somebody was sick into a pencil case and after that all they wanted to know was why it is that sick always has carrots in it. What lesson could that have been turned into?

A A General Science lesson: in which children learn how to identify common materials by sorting them into groups according to simple properties.

Q What if children then get distracted by a book about ghosts, and spectres and stuff like that?

A Think about it. Think about importance of myth, fable and the oral tradition in the context of a school's literacy strategy.

Miss Twigg had been going to say, "We came here to learn about history not to listen to some old biddy prattle on about haunted mines." But she didn't.

She said,

Why don't we go to Mrs Batty's cottage and ask her to tell us what life was like when she was a girl? I'm sure she'll have some interesting tales to tell.

"You mean about ghosts?" said Terry.
"Maybe," said Miss Twigg.
"Spectres that haunt the canal towpath in the dead of night?" said Mark.
"Perhaps," said Miss Twigg.
"Headless monsters rattling chains and wailing, 'Woarr, woarr, woarr'?" said Craig.
"Well, I'm not sure about that," said Miss Twigg.
Miss Twigg wanted to know what we thought of her idea.
We thought it was a brilliant idea.

So that's what we did.

But Mrs Batty wasn't at home.

She's up in the woods looking for Wolfgang.

Wolfgang was Mrs Batty's dog.
Mr Batty said that he'd escaped again.
He said, "You could go and help her
find him. *If you've got nothing better to
do.*"
Miss Twigg put her hands on her hips
and said, "As it happens—"
Then stopped.
Because she'd remembered something
she'd read in her really useful book.

It was the chapter entitled

> ### CITIZENSHIP
>
> A good teacher should take every opportunity to encourage the children in his or her class to perform spontaneous acts of kindness. They should be encouraged to help friends, neighbours and family, and in particular those members of their community who are disadvantaged such as the elderly, the infirm, Stoke City supporters and *people who live up the woods in old tumbling-down stone cottages that don't have the benefit of an inside toilet.*

"As it happens," said Miss Twigg.

And that's what we did.

But by the time we'd got up into the woods the sun had gone in, the air had turned cold and Barry, Craig, Terry and Mark had gone off the idea of being good citizens.

"It might be a *big* dog," said Barry. "And I don't like big dogs."

"It could be a fierce dog," said Craig. "And I don't care for fierce dogs."

"With a name like Wolfgang it could be a WOLF," said Mark.

And nobody was keen to be wandering around a big gloomy wood looking for a big fierce dog that might be a wolf.

So they were rather relieved when Danny Bloor said,

Please, Miss. The storm's coming. We ought to find somewhere to shelter.

Nearby was an old mine building.
Miss Twigg said we could shelter in
there.
Then changed her mind.

Yuck! It's disgusting!

Miss Twigg said the old mine building
was unsuitable.
She said it was probably infested with
rats and goodness knows what else.
She said not to worry. It would
probably only be a passing shower
anyway.
She said it was the wrong time of year
for a thunderstorm.
She said we would make our way back
to the Canal Heritage Museum and take
shelter there.
She might have been going to say
something else but didn't. Because just
at that moment there came a blinding

Miss Twigg didn't reply.

And if she had have done Dan wouldn't have heard her anyway because a few seconds later there came a deafening

But Miss Twigg didn't reply.
Because she wasn't there.

And neither was anyone else.
They were all in the old mine building.

said Miss Twigg.
"Much better than being in that boring old heritage centre, isn't it?"

Nobody said anything.
"Would anyone like to play a game of
I-spy?" said Miss Twigg.

Nobody wanted to play a game of I-spy.
"How about we have a sing-song?" said
Miss Twigg.
Nobody felt like singing.
"Does anybody know any good knock-
knock jokes?" said Miss Twigg.
Nobody knew any good knock-knock
jokes.
"Well, what *do* you want to do?" said
Miss Twigg.
"I want to go home," said Craig, Barry,
Terry and Mark.
"Well, you can't. We're stuck here and
we've got to find a way of passing the
time."

I could tell 'em a
few stories if you like.

It was Mrs Batty.

"I know lots of stories," she said. "True stories about strange things what 'ave 'appened 'ereabouts. There's the story of the Phantom Odious Lock-keeper, the legend of the Legless Lead-smelter and then there's my favourite. A spine-tingling tale entitled . . .

THE WAILING BOGGART OF THE BLACK PIG MINE!

"Oh, splendid!" said Miss Twigg.

An oral history lesson!

MEANWHILE, OUT IN THE STORM

Danny Bloor was searching for Mrs Batty's dog

when he noticed something interesting.

The trail of pawprints went along a path, down some steps and then along another path which led right up to

the entrance to a tunnel which led to
the very heart of

in the old mine building Mrs Batty
was coming to the end of her story.
"So remember, children," she said.
"Don't ever go near the Black Pig Mine.
Because if you do dare go near that
accursed tunnel especially after a storm
'as reeked its 'avoc on the land you may
still be 'orrified to hear the cry of the
'orrible Wailing Boggart.
A strange unearthly cry what sounds a
bit like this."

WOARR!

"Well, that was a very interesting story, wasn't it, children?" said Miss Twigg. "You enjoyed that. Didn't you?"

the rain had stopped.
But Miss Twigg was still talking.
And Mrs Batty was still having to listen.

Yes. I do take your point.

Mrs Batty said she'd love to hear more
about the importance of myth, fable
and the oral tradition in the context
of a school's literacy strategy
but . . .

I need to go and look for my dog.

And that's what she did.
But when Miss Twigg said, "Right,
children. We'll go and have a closer
look at this old Black Pig mine tunnel,
shall we?" Mrs Batty came running
back again and said, "No!! *I wouldn't
do that*!"

She didn't say *why* it was dangerous.
She didn't get the chance.
Because just then Paul Dimbley shouted,
"Miss! Come quick! It's Dan."

We all followed Paul along a path,
down some steps and then along
another path until we came to

Dan's umbrella.

But where was Dan?
"Maybe he's been blinded by lightning
and fallen into the canal," said Karen.
"Maybe he's been deafened by thunder
and plunged into a mine shaft!" said
Julie.
Craig Soapy pointed towards the
entrance to the Black Pig Mine and
said, "More likely he's been dragged
into that accursed tunnel by the Wailing
Boggart!"
"Oh, don't be ridiculous, Craig!" said
Miss Twigg. "There's no such thing.
That was just a made-up story Mrs
Batty told you.

"There's nothing in that tunnel,
absolutely nothing. It's just an old
empty mine tunnel." Then she said,
"Look. I'll show you." She strode over
to the tunnel, poked her head inside and
called,

And something deep in the heart of
the Black Pig Mine replied . . .

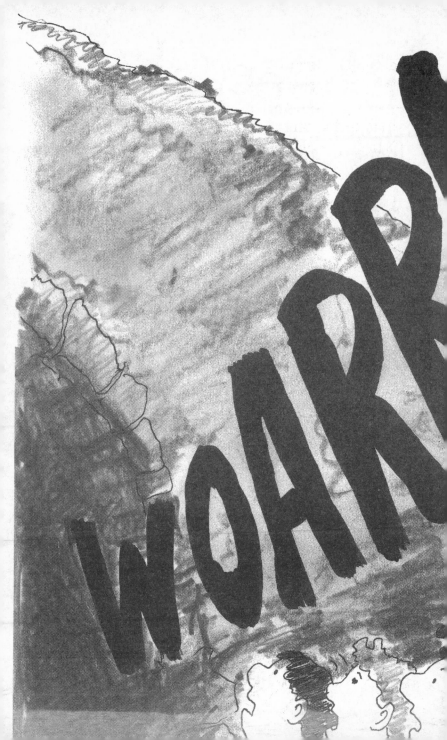

EEEeeeek!

shrieked Craig. "It's the phantom of the Odious Lock-keeper!"

OOOooorh!

shouted Terry. "It's the ghost of the Legless Lead-smelter!"

Aaaaarhh!

screamed Mark. "It's the Wailing Boggart of the Black Pig Mine!"

"Excuse me, Miss," said Karen Smart.

I was just wondering.

Seeing as you're a teacher you probably know more about the sort of things that usually make Woarring noises in old mine tunnels than Craig, Terry or Mark do. So I wonder if you'd mind telling me...

What do *you* think it is?

Miss Twigg didn't reply.
She was thinking what she should say.
She was thinking about a chapter in her
Really Useful Book which was entitled

DEALING WITH CHILDREN'S FEARS

What to say – and what not to say.

Q If a class of children are sheltering from a thunderstorm in an old, deserted, dark (probably rat-infested) mine building what should a good teacher do to stop them from being scared?

A Firstly the teacher should pretend that she thinks it's a really cosy old, deserted, dark (probably rat-infested) mine building. Next she should suggest things they could do to pass the time such as tell knock-knock jokes, have a sing song, or play I-spy. (NOTE: On no account should the teacher let some old biddy tell them scary stories about a Wailing Boggart that goes Woarrr! Woarr! Woarrr!)

Q What if a teacher forgets what you just said about letting an old biddy tell the children ghost stories and then a bit later they're outside a mine tunnel and something does go, "Woarr! Woarr! Woarr!" and the teacher thinks, "Arggghhh!! It really is the Wailing Boggart" and then one of the children says, "Please, Miss. What do you think it is?" What should a good teacher say?

A The teacher's main concern should be to get the children to a place of safety without causing undue alarm or panic. To do this the teacher must convince the children that the Woaarr! Woarrr! Woarr! noise was made by something friendly and entirely harmless.

Q Like what, for instance?

A I don't know, do I? You'll just have to use your imagination.

Miss Twigg had got a good imagination.
She said, "Listen to me, everybody.
That noise we just heard. I think I know
what it was."

It was the sound of a naughty little
baby bunny rabbit getting angry and
making a terrible fuss because her
mummy wouldn't let her go out to
play until she'd eaten all her tea.

She was probably going to suggest
that it might be rather a nice idea for
us all to go and have a look at a *really
interesting tree* that she'd just noticed
three miles away – but she didn't get the
chance.

Because just then Karen Smart said,

"Oh NO!" shouted Miss Twigg.

But it wasn't.
It was Danny Bloor.
He said,

Just look who
I've found.

He was in the tunnel
hiding from the storm.
He was really frightened.

Miss Twigg gave Dan a big hug. "I'm so
glad you're safe. We were all worried
about you. We thought you'd been . . ."
"Been what?" said Dan.
"Been . . . er . . . frightened," said Miss
Twigg.

"Frightened of what?" said Dan.
"The dark," said Craig.
"The thunder and lightning," said Terry.
"The Wailing Boggart," said Mark.
Dan hadn't been afraid of the dark, or thunder and lightning, and he'd no idea what Mark was talking about.
After Barry had explained about the Wailing Boggart, Dan laughed and said, "Well, he wasn't in there today."
"But if the Boggart wasn't in there," said Karen Smart, "what on earth made that terrifying woarrring sound?"
"Oh that," said Dan, "was probably Wolfgang."

It was very echoey in the tunnel. Wasn't it, Wolfie?

Woarr.

When Mrs Batty arrived and saw that Wolfgang had been found she was pleased and very relieved. She said, "The little scoundrel's always runnin' off. 'E'll come to 'arm one of these days if 'e's not careful. Where'd you find 'im?"

He was hiding in the tunnel, said Dan.

On hearing this Mrs Batty suddenly went all peculiar.
"Oh no! Not the Black Pig tunnel," she cried. "I can't bear to think about what could have happened. The mere thought of him being in there makes my blood run cold!"
"Why?" said Miss Twigg.
"I've already told you," said Mrs Batty.

"Nonsense," said Miss Twigg.

She was probably going to tell Mrs Batty that it was very wrong of her to go about frightening people with tales about how the Black Pig Mine tunnel was terribly dangerous because it was haunted by a hideously horrible Wailing Boggart.
But she didn't get the chance.
Because a few seconds later . . .

The tunnel collapsed!

we had a special assembly.
Mrs Batty had come to school to thank
Dan for risking his life to save
Wolfgang.
And to bring him a present.

By way of a small reward.

A reward he justly deserves.

Mrs Batty said she hadn't had a chance
to ask Dan what sort of things he did in
his spare time. "What with the tunnel
collapsin' an' all that."
But she could remember when her sons
were Dan's age. "An' I'm pretty sure it's
the sort of thing a boy like you will like."

Dan unwrapped the parcel and opened the box.

When he saw what was inside he said,

Thank you very much. You're very kind.

Mr Warrilow agreed. He said that Mrs Batty was indeed very kind. He said that a pump-action mega-blaster water pistol was a perfect present for a boy like Dan. He probably would have said a lot more but Miss Twigg said, "Excuse me, Mr Warrilow."

These boys have got something they want to say.

"What d'you think?" said Mark.

"I think it's wonderful!" said Dan.
"Just what I've always wanted."

An embroidery set with frame,
instruction book, and sixteen
different coloured threads.

THE END

LUCKY
LILY

When Miss Twigg chooses Lily to perform a special task at the school fashion show she says

I must be blessed with good fortune.

But Nicola is not so happy.

Will everything go according to plan?

Not if I can help it!